For the Barksdale family
—M. R.

Hey, Jude, this one's for you!
—E. C.

Farrar Straus Giroux Books for Young Readers
An imprint of Macmillan Publishing Group, LLC
120 Broadway, New York, NY 10271 • mackids.com

Our books may be purchased in bulk for promotional, educational, or business use.
Please contact your local bookseller or the Macmillan Corporate and Premium Sales Department
at (800) 221-7945 ext. 5442 or by email at MacmillanSpecialMarkets@macmillan.com.

Library of Congress Cataloging-in-Publication Data is available.

First edition, 2023
Book design by Asher Caswell
Color separations by Embassy Graphics
Printed in China by RR Donnelley Asia Printing Solutions Ltd.,
Dongguan City, Guangdong Province

ISBN 978-0-374-39014-3
1   3   5   7   9   10   8   6   4   2

On the Fourth of July

FIREWORKS

Maggie C. Rudd   Pictures by **Elisa Chavarri**

Farrar Straus Giroux • New York

On the Fourth of July
when the sun sinks low,

when the
sparklers come out
and the fireflies glow.

When the cookouts are over
and the pool gates are closed,

when coolers are emptied
and sunburns show.
Then . . .

We'll walk from our houses.
We'll parade into town.
We've been waiting all day
for the sun to go down.

We'll ride high on shoulders.
We'll race on our bikes.
We'll lift flags above us
and wave stars and stripes.

We'll blow horns and fly streamers.
"Let freedom ring!"

"Happy Birthday, America!"
the people will sing.

We'll lay out our quilts
or we'll perch on our cars.
We'll set up our lawn chairs
and look to the stars.

We'll laugh with our neighbors.
We'll chat with our friends.

Then a cannon will **BOOM!**
And the fireworks begin.

A bright **SILVER** shower
will *glitter* and *glow*.

And just as it dims,
another **EXPLODES!**

RED sends out sparkles

and **GOLD** paints the sky.

BLUE scatters and dances

as **PURPLE** sails by.

Flung from a paintbrush
on a canvas of sky,

They POP! and they CRACKLE!

They ECHO! and POUND!

They **SING!** and they **WHISTLE!**

They **JUMP!** and they **BOUND!**

A pause near the end
sends a hush through the streets.

The finale begins
and folks leap to their feet.

Like a song full of spirit.
Like birds, how they glide.

The people will look on
with wonder, with pride.

And when it's all over,
the celebration will end.

We'll pack up our blankets,
wave goodbye to our friends.

We'll take our time leaving.
We'll gaze at the sky.

We'll crawl into back seats
and rub tired eyes.

We'll hold hands with our parents
and swing from their arms.

We'll head back to our houses,
our fields, and our farms.

We'll lie in our beds
when July Fourth is through.

And we'll dream of the colors
red, white, and blue.